VAMPIRES IN LITERATURE

Bridget Heos

rosen publishing's
rosen central

New York

For my friend Jen and her beautiful family

Published in 2012 by The Rosen Publishing Group, Inc.
29 East 21st Street, New York, NY 10010

First Edition

Library of Congress Cataloging-in-Publication Data

Heos, Bridget.
Vampires in literature / Bridget Heos.
    p. cm.—(Vampires)
Includes bibliographical references and index.
ISBN 978-1-4488-1225-7 (library binding)
ISBN 978-1-4488-2228-7 (pbk.)
ISBN 978-1-4488-2237-9 (6-pack)
1. Vampires in literature. I. Title.
PN56.V3H46 2012
809'.93375—dc22

                                                          2010011077

Manufactured in Malaysia

CPSIA Compliance Information: Batch #S11YA: For further information, contact Rosen Publishing, New York, New York, at 1-800-237-9932.

On the cover: Left: Bram Stoker, the author of *Dracula*, helped to usher in what we associate with vampires today. Right: Anne Rice, the author of the Vampire Chronicles series.

CONTENTS

INTRODUCTION

FROM bloodsucking monsters to teenage heartthrobs, vampires have come a long way. They are no longer evil by definition. But neither are they human. They must drink blood. That makes them different.

But what makes them so popular in literature? Look up vampire books in an online bookstore, and you'll find tens of thousands of titles—many intended for a young adult (YA) or middle grade audience. For teenagers, *The Vampire Diaries*, Twilight series, and Vampire Academy books are popular. Younger students can choose from *The Chronicles of Vladimir Tod*, *My Sister the Vampire*, *Cirque du Freak*, and many others. A wide range of manga, comic books, and graphic novels also depict vampires.

This book will trace the popularity of vampires in literature—from the dawn of horror novels to the present popularity of YA titles. We'll explore how each story offers a unique portrait, while drawing on old myths and legends. We'll see how authors address the question of whether vampires are always bad, usually bad, or, like humans, either good or bad. This is linked to how they seek blood.

Vampires have come a long way from their monster days. As of January 2010, Stephenie Meyer's romantic Twilight series had sold eighty-five million copies.

In the Twilight series, most vampires are vicious killers. But the vampires who live in Forks are determined to keep their humanity. So they hunt animals instead of humans. In the Vampire Academy series, vampires fall into the category of Moroi, good vampires who feed off blood donors, and Strigoi, evil vampires who attack people. In *The Vampire Diaries*, vampires behave however they did as humans. That's why Stefan's brother Damon, who was bad as a human, is an evil vampire.

Beyond blood, other folklore surrounds vampires. Authors interpret this in many intriguing ways. For instance, there is the question of sunlight.

Count Dracula was paralyzed during the daylight hours. The vampires in *The Vampire Diaries* can go out in sunlight if they wear a special ring. Otherwise, they burn. And in *Twilight*, the sun doesn't hurt the vampires. Rather, it makes them sparkle. Instead of becoming creatures of the night, they move to Forks, Washington, where it rains most of the time.

Then there is the bigger question: what is vampirism? Is it a disease, as is the case in *I Am Legend* and *Peeps*? Or is it an alternate form of being, like angels? Are all vampires damned, or does that depend on how they live?

For humans, the question is: why are we so intrigued by vampires? Perhaps it is because they look like us but are not quite human. They live forever. They avoid sunlight. They often have superhuman strength and speed. At the same time, they often hate being vampires because they must either fight to remain humanlike or surrender to being monsters.

CHAPTER 1

VAMPIRES ARE MONSTERS: EARLY WRITINGS

SINCE ancient times, people have told stories of creatures that suck blood. These creatures helped explain deaths from contagious illness. Their stories were also warnings, encouraging people to follow religious teachings and avoid evil.

The Greeks told of the goddess Sekhmet, who was sent by the god Ra to punish humans for their evildoings. She went overboard, killing everyone and becoming drunk on their blood.

In Latin America, the camazotz, or "death bat," had a male body, a bat head, and a thirst for blood. Tlahuelpuchi was a witch who sucked the blood of children. She could be warded off with garlic and onions.

In Eastern Europe, vampires included the Slavic Upir, a bloodsucking corpse with two hearts and two souls; the Bosnian lampire, who rose from the dead to spread disease; and the Bulgarian vampire, a human-looking monster who rose from the grave to wreak havoc at night. Today's vampires are rooted in these Eastern European myths. Here's why.

In 1732, a report was released about the investigation of vampires in Serbia. A man named Arnold Paole

Mammalia Pl. 1

Desmodus D'Orbigny.

Vampire bats, illustrated here in *The Zoology of the Voyage of the HMS Beagle*, suck the blood of animals but not humans. Still, this bloodthirsty species may explain why bats are associated with vampire legends.

was believed to have been bitten by a vampire, died, and risen to kill others. Townspeople dug him up and staked him through the heart. Other corpses that were dug up were also believed to be too well preserved. Hence, they, too, must have been vampires. After the story was published in Belgrade, other European publications picked it up. It ran in the *London Journal* and *Gentleman's Magazine*. English people were now familiar with vampires.

Meanwhile, with the publication of Horace Walpole's *Castle of Otranto* and Ann Radcliffe's *Mysteries of Udolpho* in 1765, the gothic novel was born. The gothic novel, like all horror, is meant to terrify its readers. It features haunted houses, supernatural creatures, stereotyped characters, suspense, and a spooky atmosphere. Walpole's and Radcliffe's books were not about vampires, but the undead would eventually become among the most popular characters in the horror genre.

The first modern vampire story was written by John Polidori. Polidori was the poet Lord George Byron's personal physician and traveling companion. One night, the two were with Mary Wollstonecraft and her husband-to-be, Percy Shelley. They passed the time by telling ghost stories. Wollstonecraft told the story that would become *Frankenstein*. Byron told a story in which a man was dying and told his traveling companion not to tell anyone of his death.

Polidori decided to finish Byron's story. He used Byron's premise but turned the dying man, Lord Ruthven, into a vampire. Written as a likeness of Lord Byron, he was rich, handsome, and charismatic—which made him dangerously manipulative. In 1819, *The Vampyre* was published in the *New Monthly Magazine*.

VAMPYRES ARE ARISTOCRATS

Physician John Polidori, seen here in an oil painting by F. G. Gainsford, wrote *The Vampyre*. Its aristocratic villain would influence vampire stories for years.

The Vampyre told the story of Aubrey, a young, idealistic man who becomes enamored with Lord Ruthven, a stranger in town. When Aubrey travels with Ruthven, he learns of his bad character. He gambles to win against poor fathers but doesn't care if he loses to rich men, for instance.

Aubrey leaves Ruthven and travels to Greece, where he meets the beautiful Ianthe. When she tells him about vampires, Aubrey begins to think Ruthven is a vampire. One night, Ianthe is attacked and killed by a vampire. Afterward, Aubrey contracts a bad fever.

Ruthven returns to nurse him back to health. Aubrey decides Ruthven is not a vampire, and they travel together again. When the two are attacked

VAMPIRES: THE GOOD, THE BAD, AND THE UGLY

GOOD

Stefan (*The Vampire Diaries*)...tries to protect Elena from his evil brother.

Aidan (*Forever and the Night*)...feeds off bad guys, saving children in the process, and sees in Neely the woman predicted to save him.

Bill (Sookie Stackhouse series)...lives among humans so that he'll keep his humanity and protects Sookie from other vampires.

Edward (Twilight series)...forsakes human blood and tries to protect Bella from himself and his family by breaking up with her.

Dmitri (*Vampire Academy*)...a dhampir, he teaches Rose fighting moves that will allow her to fight Strigoi—and in the process falls in love with her.

BAD

Lord Ruthven (*The Vampyre*)...kills Aubrey's girlfriend and then his sister, driving his friend mad in the process.

Dracula (*Dracula*)...imprisons his houseguest, Jonathan Harker, and then tries to steal his fiancée by turning her into a vampire.

Damon (*The Vampire Diaries*)...kills a teacher in the school haunted house, framing his brother for the crime.

Aro (*New Moon*)...lures tourists into his lair, pretending to offer a historical vampire tour—then, with his fellow Volterra, eats them.

UGLY

Varney (*Varney the Vampire*)...One of the last old-school vampires, he is a grotesque monster, rather than one of the handsome modern-day vampires.

by robbers, Ruthven suffers a mortal wound. He makes Aubrey promise not to tell anyone of his sins—or his death.

Later, Aubrey learns that Ruthven is still alive . . . and courting his sister. He is bound not to tell her that Ruthven should be dead. Keeping the secret literally drives Aubrey crazy, and he is locked up in his bedroom. When he finally breaks free to warn her, it is too late. Ruthven has killed his sister and escaped.

Ruthven was a groundbreaking vampire. At the time, most folklore portrayed vampires as ugly monsters. Ruthven was a monster—but he was also handsome and rich. In that way, *The Vampyre* set the stage for aristocratic vampires like Dracula. Even today, vampires in literature tend to be well off.

In *Twilight*, the teenage vampires living in Forks all drive expensive cars, thanks to their adoptive father, who has been a successful surgeon for hundreds of years. Ann Rice's Marius enjoys the best of everything—whether in ancient Rome or during the Renaissance—because he hunts evildoers and steals their gold. There are exceptions, of course. In the Vampire Academy books, the good vampires—who don't live forever—are as economically diverse as humans. And in *Peeps*, those infected with the vampire virus often lose everything as they descend into madness.

Like Lord Ruthven, vampires are also typically polite and polished, having grown up in a more formal era. And they are usually strikingly beautiful. For instance, in the Blue Bloods series, supermodels are vampires.

Although *The Vampyre* influenced vampire literature for years to come, it didn't spark a vampire craze. At the time, ghost stories were more popular. Of the small number of vampire books that were published, not all were scary or serious. Paul Feval's *La Ville-Vampire* parodied the

No. 1.]   Nos. 2, 3 and 4 are Presented, Gratis, with this No.   [Price 1d.

VARNEY THE VAMPIRE, OR THE FEAST OF BLOOD

A ROMANCE OF EXCITING INTEREST.

BY THE AUTHOR OF

"...RCHANT'S DAUGHTER."

..., AND ALL BOOKSELLERS.

As seen on the cover of this penny dreadful, Varney the Vampire was an old-school vampire. He was neither handsome nor aristocratic. He was simply a monster.

gothic novels of Ann Radcliffe. The main character was even named Ann Radcliffe.

The two most popular vampire novels at the time were *Varney the Vampire* and *Carmilla*. *Varney the Vampire*, written by James Malcolm Rymer in the 1840s, is about a vampire who preys on young women, turning them into vampires. It was a penny dreadful, which means it sold in cheap chapter installments. The title character, Varney, feels badly about who he is, making him a sympathetic character. But make no mistake: he is a monster—both inside and out. Ugly and unrefined, he harkened back to traditional vampire folklore.

In 1872, *Carmilla*, by Sheridan Le Fanu, followed in Polidori's tradition of aristocratic vampires. It tells the story of Laura, who lives in an Austrian castle. She's dreamed of the same woman since childhood. As an adult, she witnesses a carriage accident. One of the women involved is the woman of Laura's dreams. The stranger, named Carmilla, stays at Laura's house. During that time, Laura grows ill as she repeatedly dreams of a cat biting her. Carmilla turns out to be a long-dead countess who is now a vampire. She has been feeding on Laura while she sleeps. The countess's corpse is dug up, and a stake is driven through her heart.

The castle setting and the idea of a vampire stalking a particular person may have influenced Bram Stoker as he wrote *Dracula*. *Dracula*, in turn, would influence writers for decades to come.

CHAPTER 2

VAMPIRES WEAR TUXEDOS: DRACULA

BORN in 1847, Bram Stoker grew up in Ireland during the potato famine. At this time, many Irish families died of starvation or sickness because of failed crops. However, his family (Stoker was the third of seven children) was secure because his father worked for the government. Stoker was a sickly child and wasn't expected to live long. He had to stay in bed for most of his young life. To pass the time, his mother told him scary folktales of screaming banshees and fairies who drank children's blood.

Stoker surprised everyone when he not only recovered but grew to be big and strong. He was a nice, friendly guy, unlike the dark stories he would later write. He studied math and science in college and then worked as a clerk—an office worker who handles paperwork. At the same time, he became a volunteer theater critic for the local newspaper. The job changed his life.

He became friends with the actor Henry Irving, who is believed to be the prototype for Count Dracula. Irving was handsome, charismatic,

Bram Stoker, photographed in 1890 (seven years before *Dracula* was published), was by all accounts a happy, friendly guy, unlike his dark novels.

and temperamental. When he took over the Lyceum Theater in London, he asked Stoker to be the manager. In 1878, Stoker married Florence Balcombe and moved to London.

While managing the Lyceum Theater, he wrote part-time. His first book, *Under the Sunset*, published in 1881, was a collection of children's fairy tales, many of them scary and surreal. His first novel, *The Snake's Pass*, published in 1890, told the story of an Englishman who travels to a mysterious Irish town. There, he searches for legendary treasure, tries to outwit a bad guy, and battles a deadly bog. The same year, Stoker began writing *Dracula*, a novel seven years in the making.

While writing *Dracula*, Stoker spent time in Whitby, England. There, he was inspired by St. Mary's Cathedral and the ruins of Whitby Abbey— both built in the 1100s. The architecture in the book, particularly Dracula's castle, was based on this style. Whitby is also the setting of much of the book.

Beyond his surroundings, Stoker drew inspiration from his research. From the library, he checked out *An Account of the Principalities of Wallachia and Moldavia*, which describes the region of Romania where part of Dracula is set. He also read about Vlad Dracula (Vlad the Impaler), a fifteenth-century Walachian ruler known for his brutal impaling of enemies— both real and imagined.

Vlad Dracula inspired at least the name of the fictional Count Dracula. Stoker wrote in his notes that Dracula meant "son of the devil." (It also means "son of the dragon.") Whether Vlad the Impaler inspired more than just the name of Stoker's character is unknown. When Stoker began working on the novel, he called the main character Count Wampyr. It's possible that he simply needed a wicked name for a character he had already imagined.

Vlad Dracula was a fifteenth-century Walachian ruler known for impaling his enemies. It is unknown whether Bram Stoker based Count Dracula on this real-life person or only borrowed his name.

On the other hand, there may be a stronger tie between Vlad Dracula and Count Dracula. Stoker's friend Armenius Vanbury was a professor at Budapest University and a scholar of Romanian history, including Vlad the Impaler. Through him, Stoker may have learned more about Vlad the Impaler. In fact, a character in Dracula mentions a man named Armenius and calls him a wise scholar.

Whatever the inspiration for Count Dracula (or if he simply sprung from the author's imagination), he became one of the most memorable villains ever.

VAMPIRES ARE TERRIBLE HOSTS

Dracula begins with an excerpt from the journals of Jonathan Harker. Traveling to Transylvania for work, he stays with Count Dracula. Harker suspects that something isn't right with Dracula: He never eats or drinks, and he doesn't appear in mirrors. When Harker cuts himself shaving, Dracula nearly pounces on him. Worst of all, Dracula has locked all the doors of the castle, making Harker a prisoner.

At last, Harker escapes but becomes ill and is unable to return to England. Meanwhile, Dracula arrives in Whitby, where he attacks Mina's friend Lucy. Lucy is turned into a vampire. Mina is also attacked by Dracula but does not become a vampire. Harker and three of Lucy's friends, Quincey Morris, Arthur Holmwood, and Abraham Van Helsing, pursue Dracula to destroy him and stop the spread of vampirism.

The novel *Dracula* has an interesting format. Composed of diary passages, letters, and newspaper articles, it tells the story as if someone has gathered evidence in a strange case. This, along with the modern medicine used in the book (Dr. Seward does a blood transfusion; Van Helsing is a doctor skilled at diagnosing rare diseases) makes the story seem like it could be true.

In spite of the skilled writing and compelling story, *Dracula* wasn't popular when it first came out in 1897. It got mixed reviews, and Bram Stoker didn't make much money off it. In fact, when he died in 1912, he and his wife were broke.

Bram Stoker spent time in Whitby, England, while writing *Dracula*. Whitby Abbey and St. Mary's Cathedral, shown here, inspired the architecture in the book.

Things changed in 1922, when a German filmmaker, F. W. Murnau, made *Nosferatu: A Symphony of Horror*. It was an unauthorized adaptation of *Dracula*. When Florence Stoker sued the filmmaker, newspaper readers followed the lawsuit. The movie and the press coverage revived *Dracula*. In the 1930s, Stoker sold the rights to the story to Universal. This authorized version of *Dracula*, starring Bela Lugosi, sealed the character's image in people's minds and ensured the story's popularity for years to come.

According to the *Guinness Book of World Records*, Dracula is the most frequently portrayed character in horror films. Today, the most prestigious award for horror is known as the Bram Stoker Award.

Bram Stoker popularized many vampire symbols that he adapted from folklore. Although Dracula lived in a castle and not in a grave, as did vampires in folklore, he slept in a coffin from dawn to dusk. He didn't appear in mirrors, which coincides with a superstition that soulless beings are not reflected in mirrors. The crucifix and garlic repelled him, which also reflect folk beliefs. And, in keeping with traditional vampire lore, he could be killed by driving a stake through his heart.

Authors have adopted some of these conventions and explained others away. For instance, in *Peeps*, the main character says that vampires are repelled by crucifixes only if they were devout Christians prior to becoming vampires. The reason for this is that vampirism is a sickness in which sufferers hate the things they once loved. In the book, this also explains why they avoid mirrors. Prior to becoming vampires, they liked themselves. Now their own image repels them.

While *Dracula* grew in popularity, vampire novels were few and far between. However, in pulp fiction magazines and comic books, the undead were popular characters.

Lestat de Lioncourt, played by Stuart Townsend in the movie *Queen of the Damned*, is one example of how aristocratic vampires now dominate literature.

TO BITE OR NOT TO BITE: THAT IS THE QUESTION

When Dracula drank blood from a person, he could potentially turn him or her into a vampire. That didn't happen in *The Vampyre* or *Varney the Vampire*. In those stories, the vampires killed their victims.

But in many books today, vampires can "make" new vampires. This creates a dilemma for the vampires. Do they like what they are? Would they wish it on someone else? In *The Reformed Vampire Support Group*, vampires vow not to bite other people in order to stop the spread of vampirism. In *Twilight*, Edward doesn't want to make Bella into a vampire because he considers it to be a cursed existence. Other vampires in literature purposely create new vampires. In *Peeps*, vampires spread the disease, knowing that vampires will be needed as soldiers to battle an evil force brewing within the earth. Sometimes, this decision backfires. In *Interview with the Vampire*, Lestat selfishly turns a little girl into a vampire. She deplores him for it and tries to kill him.

CHAPTER
3

VAMPIRES IN COMIC BOOKS AND PULP FICTION

THE year before *Dracula* was published, two types of popular fiction were introduced: pulp magazines and comic strips.
In 1896, the first pulp was *All-Story Magazine*. Like the penny
dreadfuls of earlier decades, it offered entertaining fiction at a
cheap price. Other magazines followed suit, often specializing
in mystery, action, or horror stories. One such horror magazine,
Weird Tales, printed a steady stream of vampire tales in the 1920s,
beginning with the story "The Hound." Vampires continued in
popularity until pulp fiction magazines were replaced
by comic books in the 1940s.

The first comic strip, *The Yellow Kid*, was published in 1896 in the *New York World* newspaper. Its
popularity encouraged other newspaper publishers to
follow suit. As more comic strips were introduced, they
reflected the humor of *The Yellow Kid*. But in the late
1920s, more serious characters, such as hard-boiled
detective Dick Tracy and Tarzan, who had been a character in pulp fiction, began appearing in comic strips.

In 1933, Max Gaines reprinted some of the
humorous comic strips in installments called *Funnies*

Amazing Stories was a pulp fiction magazine that featured bone-chilling horror stories. The once-popular genre was later usurped by comic books.

on Parade—the first comic books. Soon after, Gaines published more serious comic books, including Superman, beginning in 1937. Other publishers also came out with comic books that, like the pulp magazines, specialized in mystery, crime, romance, westerns, and, of course, superheroes. Vampires were featured in some of these, including the Dr. Occult and Batman series of the 1930s, and *Adventures into the Unknown* in the 1940s.

At the time, comic books enjoyed the popularity among kids (especially boys) that TV shows and video games do today. In the 1940s, kids especially loved comic books that featured superheroes. Unfortunately for Gaines, he sold his portion of the company in 1945, losing the rights to Superman, Wonder Woman, and other popular superheroes. He began a new company, Educational Comics (EC), which printed Bible stories, animal fables, and historical stories. Kids didn't enjoy these as much as the action-packed superhero stories. EC went into debt.

When Gaines died in 1947, his son Bill took over. That's when comic books changed. Bill made the E in EC stand for "Entertaining" instead of "Educational." At first, Gaines and artist Al Feldstein copied the Western

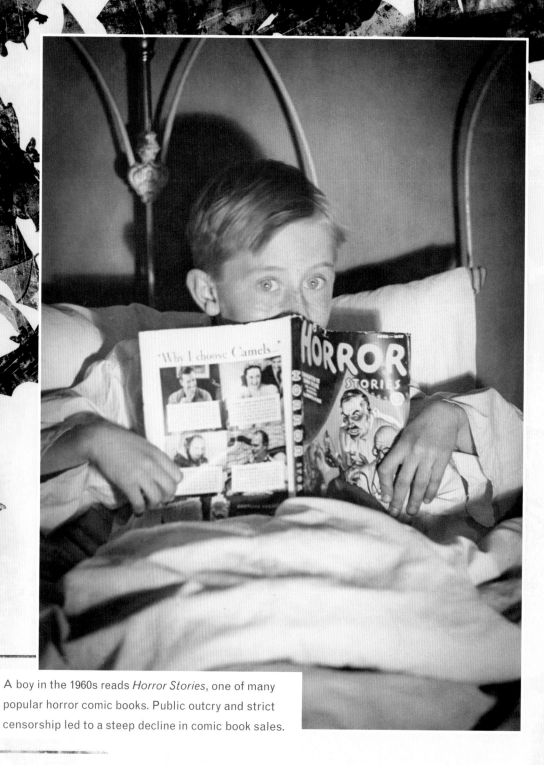

A boy in the 1960s reads *Horror Stories*, one of many popular horror comic books. Public outcry and strict censorship led to a steep decline in comic book sales.

and romance comic books that were popular at the time. Then they started a new trend in comics based on something they both liked: scary stories. In 1950, EC Comics published *The Crypt of Terror*, *The Vault of Horror*, and *The Haunt of Fear*. The horror comic book was born. Soon, other publishers copied EC Comics.

Vampires made several appearances in horror comic books. For instance, in *The Haunt of Fear*, "Grim Fairy Tale" tells the story of Sleeping Beauty, who in this version turns out to be a vampire.

EC vampires influenced a young Stephen King, who went on to be one of the most popular horror writers ever. His second published book was *'Salem's Lot*, a story about a town plagued by vampires. In the introduction to the book, he says that Dracula and EC Comics were his biggest inspirations. For instance, he recalled issues of *Tales from the Crypt* in which vampires in a diner fed on the blood of their customers.

Needless to say, horror comic books were violent, and they became more violent through the years. They were also highly visible—they were sold at newsstands alongside newspapers and magazines. Soon, public outcry over the violence led to their downfall.

THE FALL AND RISE OF COMICS

Even before horror comic books were introduced, comics were criticized by newspaper and magazine editorialists and others. The criticism mirrored that of television today: that it wasn't educational, was a waste of time, and the characters set a bad example for children. A prominent psychiatrist named Frederic Wertham took the last claim a step further. In his book *Seduction of the Innocent,* he said that comic books caused juvenile delinquency. He said horror and crime comic books warped the brains of young

The Tomb of Dracula, a 1970s Marvel comic, depicts Dracula in modern times. It was released after the censorship of comic books was softened.

people and led them into lives of violence. Many people believed this, and the public outcry over comic books became strong.

Vendors refused to sell horror titles. Bill Gaines was called before a Senate subcommittee to testify about the violence in his EC comic books. In the hopes of fighting censorship and changing public opinion, Gaines called his fellow comic book publishers to action. In 1954, the publishers formed the Comics Magazine Association of America. Instead of fighting censorship, they decided to censor themselves. The new Comics Code banned all horror, including vampires.

The Comics Code was softened in 1971, and vampires could now appear in comic books. Comic books never regained the popularity of their heyday, but they still had many loyal fans. In 1972, Marvel Comics published *The Tomb of Dracula*, which depicted Dracula in the modern world. *Blade*, a dhampir (half human, half vampire), was a vampire slayer in the series. The character was later featured in *The Nightstalkers* comic and the 1998 movie *Blade*.

Today, many comic books are targeted toward an adult audience. For instance, Stephen King is currently writing for the *American Vampire* series, to be published by the Vertigo imprint of DC Comics. It tells the

I AM LEGEND

While horror comic books were going strong, the genre almost died out in novels. In keeping with that trend, very few vampire novels were published in the 1940s and 1950s. In fact, the classic vampire book from this era, *I Am Legend*, by Richard Matheson, was classified as science fiction when it came out in 1954.

Set in the near future, a plague has killed many humans and turned others into vampires. Only one man, Robert Neville, remains, and the vampires are trying to destroy him. Explaining vampirism as a disease was a concept later used in *Peeps* and at the beginning of the Sookie Stackhouse novels.

I Am Legend was made into a 2007 movie starring Will Smith. Though science fiction, it offered a traditional view of the vampire as a monster, as opposed to some of the more sympathetic portraits of vampires in today's literature.

story of Skinner Sweet, a Wild West outlaw who becomes America's first vampire. To adapt to the American environment, he vamps out differently than Old Country vampires: he derives power from the sun and sports rattlesnake fangs. In addition, several novels, movies, and television series have been adapted into comic books, including Anne Rice's vampire books and *Buffy the Vampire Slayer*.

Vampires have also found a home in manga-style comic books and graphic novels. Manga is Japanese-style comic art. After World War II, these comics became very popular with Japanese boys and girls. (Shonen

manga targets boy readers, whereas shojo manga targets a female audience.) Its popularity has spread to America, both in translated books and in original manga by American authors.

Several manga have been translated for an English-speaking audience, including *Chibi Vampire*, *Rosario + Vampire*, and *Vampire Hunter D*. *Chibi Vampire* is about Karin, a high school vampire with strange tendencies. Instead of sucking people's blood, she injects her blood into them. For this reason, she doesn't fit in among vampires or humans. *Rosario + Vampire* is a lighthearted manga about a regular kid stuck in a high school full of vampires and other monsters. On a more serious note, *Vampire Hunter D* is set ten thousand years from now. A war with vampires has left humans living as they did in medieval times. One village hires vampire hunter D to protect them against vampires still lurking around them.

Vampire Kisses: Blood Relatives is one example of an American author adapting a novel series into a manga series. Ellen Schreiber, author of the popular YA Vampire Kisses series, was approached by her publisher HarperCollins and manga publisher TokyoPop to create a manga based on the characters in her novels, goth girl Raven and her vampire boyfriend, Alexander.

In addition to manga, other styles of graphic novels depict vampires. These include *Life Sucks*, by Jessica Abel; *Pinnochio: Vampire Slayer*, by Dustin Higgins and Van Jensen; *Baltimore, or, The Steadfast Tin Soldier and the Vampire*, by Mike Mignola and Christopher Golden; and several Buffy the Vampire Slayer titles.

CHAPTER 4

VAMPIRES ARE LIVING IN AMERICA: THE MODERN VAMPIRE

IN 1960, the book *Psycho*, by Robert Bloch, was made into a popular movie. In 1967, *Rosemary's Baby*, by Ira Levin, became a bestseller that was also made into a celebrated movie. These books kick-started the horror genre, particularly the novel.

Meanwhile, Stephen King was a young writer selling short stories to magazines. His first book, *Carrie*, about a bullied high school girl with special powers, sold in 1973. In 1975, his second novel, *'Salem's Lot*, was about vampires, a subject that had interested him since he was a boy reading comic books.

'Salem's Lot asks the question: what if Dracula visited twentieth-century America? This is a traditional vampire story, only set in a modern town. Author Ben Mears returns to his hometown of Jerusalem's Lot, Maine, to write a novel about the Marsten House, a dilapidated mansion that has haunted him since his youth. The Marsten House has been purchased by the mysterious Mr. Straker and Mr. Barlow. Soon, tragic events begin happening. One little boy disappears, and his brother dies from

In 1984, author Stephen King was photographed in a gothic setting for an American Express commercial. His second novel, *Salem's Lot*, features a traditional vampire in modern America.

an illness. Others grow ill, too. Barlow is discovered to be a vampire, and Straker, his human helper.

Barlow is an old-school vampire. He lives in a scary, old mansion. He sleeps in a coffin by day. He can hypnotize people. He is polite and aristocratic. He turns other people into vampires just to spread evil. In fact, Barlow is such a stereotypical vampire that a character named Susan laughs at herself for imagining that her life would mirror the horror films she's seen at the drive-in.

The people in the book—once attacked by a vampire—grow ill, just as they do in *Dracula*. They are not immediately dangerous. Rather, they waste away and become averse to sunlight. Interestingly, the doctors in 'Salem's Lot think the sickness might be tuberculosis. This hearkens back to an old New England superstition. People didn't know what tuberculosis was, only that it caused its victims to waste away. Tuberculosis was also highly contagious, especially in crowded places. In farmhouses where big families lived, it would spread from relative to relative, often causing multiple deaths.

From the 1600s to the 1800s, some New Englanders believed that when a family member died of consumption, he or she returned to feed on other relatives, causing them to waste away. To prevent this, people would dig up the corpse and burn the heart or sever the head.

In *'Salem's Lot*, once people are attacked and become vampires, they visit their families first. They drink their blood, turning them into vampires. Eventually, nearly everybody in town is a vampire. The reader feels some sympathy for the vampires because they didn't ask to become vampires. At the same time, they are nothing like their human incarnations. Instead, they are monsters. Ben and his fellow vampire hunters believe they are doing the vampires a favor by slaying them, thus freeing their souls.

VAMPIRES HAVE FEELINGS

The year after *'Salem's Lot* was published, Anne Rice introduced the literary world to a new kind of vampire—one that isn't necessarily evil. In *Interview with the Vampire*, published in 1976, the main character is Louis, a plantation owner in New Orleans. When the vampire Lestat turns him into a vampire, the two travel together.

Instead of hurting humans, Louis hunts rats. But in a moment of weakness, he participates in turning a little girl into a vampire. Lestat and the little girl become monsters on the prowl for their next victim. Meanwhile, Louis is more interested in books and the beautiful things in life.

Rice followed *Interview with the Vampire* with a series of vampire novels known as *The Vampire Chronicles*. *In Blood and Gold*, Marius is a vampire who sees the fall of the Roman Empire and the Renaissance. He loves art and only hunts bad people for his blood meal. In Rice's novels, Lestat makes several appearances. In *The Vampire Lestat*, he awakes in modern times and becomes a rock star. In later books, the formerly monstrous vampire tries to turn his life around.

Author Anne Rice, photographed in 1994, introduced a somewhat romantic vampire in *Interview with the Vampire*. She later became the author of religious novels.

In keeping with tradition, Rice's vampires live for hundreds of years. They have special powers, such as the ability to read minds. They must stay out of the sun. As in *Dracula*, turning someone into a vampire requires the exchange of blood.

But in many ways, Rice's vampires break tradition. They aren't affected by holy symbols. They don't always drink blood by taking innocent lives. And when they turn others into vampires, they're usually not attacking them. Rather, they're offering the gift of immortality and special powers.

Rice and other contemporary authors, such as Chelsea Quinn Yarbro, opened the door for other authors. Vampires no longer had to be monsters. They could be good guys. They could even be romantic heroes.

Romances are novels in which two people overcome obstacles to be together. Though not technically romances, Rice's novels found an audience among romance readers. Soon, that audience would have plenty of books to sink their teeth into.

In 1993, Linda Lael Miller was among the first romance novelists to portray a vampire as a romantic hero. *Forever and the Night* tells the story of vampire Aidan Tremayne. Like Marius in Rice's *Vampire Chronicles*,

THEY WERE VAMPIRES WHEN VAMPIRES WEREN'T COOL

Before the vampire craze of the 1990s and 2000s, authors were writing vampire books. Here are some of the top vampire books from the 1970s and 1980s.

- *The Dracula Tape,* 1975, by Frederick Thomas Saberhagen, gives Dracula a chance to tell his side of the story.
- *Hotel Transylvania,* 1978, by Chelsea Quinn Yarbro, kicked off the St. Germain series, about a three-thousand-year-old peaceful vampire who lives in different historical periods.
- *The Vampire Tapestry,* 1980, by Suzy McKee Charnas, tells the story of Edward Weyland, a professor whose vampirism is a biological condition.
- *Fevre Dream,* 1982, by George R. R. Martin, is about a riverboat captain who unknowingly partners with a vampire to travel the Mississippi.
- *In Those Who Hunt the Night,* 1988, by Barbara Hambly, somebody is killing the vampires of London while they sleep by day. Dr. James Asher investigates.

Aidan feeds on evildoers. In a new twist, he can travel through time, so he typically does his hunting in the past.

Aidan is lonely. As a vampire, he can't keep company with humans, and he thinks other vampires are fiends. This theme is repeated in many books, including the Twilight series and the Sookie Stackhouse novels.

Anna Paquin and Stephen Moyer portray Sookie Stackhouse and the vampire Bill Compton in the HBO series *True Blood*. The show premiered in 2008.

The main characters in these books want to maintain their humanity, so they live among humans. But this reminds them that they are not human. Caught between the human and vampire world, they live a life of eternal loneliness.

When Aidan meets Neely Wallace, he falls hopelessly in love. The idea of the tough but tenderhearted vampire took the romance world by storm. That decade, several authors began writing vampire romances.

The paranormal romance trend picked up the next decade. According to *USA Today*, in 2004, 14 percent of all romance novels were paranormal. In 2005, that increased to 20 percent. There are currently thousands of vampire romances in print.

While many romance authors take a serious approach to the vampire, others are lighthearted. In Charlaine Harris's mystery romance series, Sookie Stackhouse, a mind-reading waitress, falls in love with Bill, a vampire. In this series, vampires claim to be the victims of a sickness that makes them allergic to sunlight and garlic and dependent on blood. They demand equal rights. Sookie learns that while some vampires, like Bill, are kind and humanlike, most are pretty strange. The books were made into the HBO series *True Blood*.

Just as vampires began to be seen as romantic heroes, they were also making their mark as teenage heartthrobs.

VAMPIRES ARE FOREVER YOUNG: YOUNG ADULT LITERATURE

VAMPIRES became popular among teen readers beginning in the 1980s, when about fifty YA vampire books were published, according to *The Vampire Book* by J. Gordon Meldon. The trend may have reflected the popularity of adult vampire books such as Anne Rice's, which attracted teen as well as adult readers. Or it may have reflected the growing number of YA novels in general.

Whatever the case, the trend grew in the early 1990s, when the YA fantasy genre blossomed. More than thirty-five YA vampire books came out between 1990 and 1992 alone, according to *The Vampire Book*.

The Vampire Diaries were among the most popular of these. Four titles by L. J. Smith, *The Awakening*, *The Struggle*, *The Fury*, and *Dark Reunion*, came out in 1991.

The Awakening tells the story of Elena, a popular high school girl who falls in love with Stefan, the new boy in school. Stefan turns out to be a vampire—but a nice one. Elena reminds Stefan of Katherine, the girl he loved hundreds of years ago. His brother Damon, now an evil vampire, also loved Katherine. The love triangle ended in Katherine's demise. Back in the present, Damon spies on Stefan and Elena and notices the resemblance. The battle between the brothers for Elena's heart begins. The books have since been made into a TV drama on the CW Network.

Television and movies contributed to the teen vampire trend. In 1987, *The Lost Boys*, about a new teen in town who falls in with a rough gang of vampires, was popular among teens. *Buffy the Vampire Slayer*, which came out as a movie in 1992 and then as a TV show in 1997, became a phenomenon unto itself.

Paul Wesley, Nina Dobrev, and Ian Somerhalder portray Damon, Elena, and Stefan in the CW drama *The Vampire Diaries*, based on the popular book series.

The popular television series spawned hundreds of books based on the TV series, from comic books to novelizations to philosophy and spirituality guides. Vampires, for the most part, were evil in *Buffy* (hence the need to slay them). But there were exceptions. Angel, who Buffy fell in love with, was a good vampire. He created a dilemma for Buffy: what's a vampire slayer to do when she falls in love with a vampire?

VAMPIRES ARE GUY'S GUYS

Teen vampire novels often have a female protagonist. The following books, on the other hand, tell vampire stories from a guy's point of view:

- **Peeps,** 2005, by Scott Westerfeld. Cal Thompson carries a vampire virus that affects him only slightly. He hunts seriously ill vampires—who are dangerously insane—to get them off the streets. When Cal realizes that certain vampires are being allowed to roam freely, he investigates why.
- **Vampire High,** 2008, by Douglas Rees. Bad grades force Cody Elliot to transfer to Vlad Dracul Magnet School, a high school populated by vampires and werewolves.
- **Night Runner,** 2009, by Max Turner. Zach Thomson, allergic to sunlight and all foods except strawberry smoothies, lives in a mental institute. When a stranger crashes through the doors and tells him to run, he goes on a journey to find out what ails him.

In the following decade, vampires would become the hottest trend in YA books. Authors like Stephenie Meyer created their own vampire lore—or offered new twists on traditional ideas.

VAMPIRES SPARKLE

YA vampire books of the new millennium ranged in genre from action to science fiction to chick lit to romance.

In 2003, Ellen Schreiber kicked off her Vampire Kisses series, in which the goth-girl main character Raven wants to be a vampire. When Alexander Sterling moves to town, she thinks her dream might come true. *Vampire Kisses* is a story of love and friendship.

Then came the most famous vampire novels of the decade: the Twilight series. Stephenie Meyer's series began as a dream. A vampire and a human girl were discussing how they were falling in love. That was a problem. The scent of the girl's blood was irresistible to the vampire, and he was tempted to devour her. After the dream, Meyer wrote about the couple nightly until the *Twilight* manuscript was complete. She didn't name the couple right away. Eventually, she chose Edward because it was a romantic but old-fashioned name and Isabella because that's what she wanted to name a daughter.

Twilight, the first book of the saga, was published in 2005. It begins with Bella Swan moving to Forks to live with her father. There, she meets Edward Cullen, a boy who seems to hate her. In fact, he is dangerously drawn to her. They begin dating, which creates problems. It is a vampire's nature to attack people for their blood. Edward and his clan hunt animals instead, but they are still tempted by human blood.

Prior to writing *Twilight*, Meyer wasn't a big fan of vampires. That is, she had read few vampire novels (not even *Dracula*!) and seen few, if any, vampire movies. However, *Twilight* includes much of the old vampire lore, including the fact that vampires can "make" another vampire by sucking some of the person's blood (too much and the vampire will kill the victim). And, as in many vampire stories, Edward and his kind have superpowers—including super speed and strength, and, in some cases, clairvoyance, or the ability to read minds. Amid the old lore, readers found in *Twilight* a fresh love story: Edward genuinely

English actor Robert Pattinson, photographed at the 2009 Cannes Film Festival, became a heartthrob when he played Edward in The Twilight Saga movies.

loves Bella, but his love threatens to devour her because of his bloodlust.

The star-crossed lovers entranced readers. As of January 2010, eighty-five million copies of novels in the Twilight series had sold world-wide. The series had been translated into fifty languages, made into highly anticipated movies, and a graphic novel series was in the works.

While fans couldn't get enough of *Twilight*, for some the saga represented the antithesis of what a vampire should be. Edward is sensitive and full of angst—a far cry from the confident, heartless vampires of old. Barely Digital, a Web site that parodies pop culture, created a video poking fun at modern vampires. In it, an old-school vampire laments that the vampires of today are too emotional and whiny. And he sets the record straight: Vampires don't sparkle in the sun—they burn.

While the vampire in the video is sick of the newfangled vampires, readers are not. Series painting vampires in a positive light continue to draw readers. *Blue Bloods*, by Melissa de la Cruz, is about students at a wealthy Manhattan school who are vampires. *House of Night*, by P. C. Cast and Kristin Cast, is about Zoey Redbird, who is not only a vampire but also one linked to a goddess. L. J. Smith also returned to the vampire scene with the Night World series, about a secret society of otherworldly creatures, including vampires.

Author Richelle Mead introduced one of the most interesting vampire worlds. In her series, beginning with *Vampire Academy* in 2008, there are Moroi, who are civilized vampires, and Strigoi, evil vampires who live forever. Dhampirs—half vampire and half human—protect Moroi from Strigoi. At the Vampire Academy, Dhampir Rose protects Lissa, a Moroi princess with unusual powers. When Lissa is threatened,

Melissa de La Cruz, author of the YA Blue Bloods series, signs books in 2004. The books depict upper-crust New York families who are, in fact, vampires.

Rose must find the culprit . . . while trying not to fall in love with her dhampir mentor, Dmitri.

Not all teen vampires are good guys. Rachel Caine's Morganville Vampires series, beginning with *Glass Houses* in 2006, tells the story of Claire Danvers, a gifted student who attends college in a town run by vampires . . . and not romantic ones either. These guys are monsters, and the people who reside in Morganville must bend to their will.

CHAPTER 6

VAMPIRES ARE SOMETIMES SWEET: CHILDREN'S AND MIDDLE GRADE VAMPIRES

SINCE the early 1800s, fantasy and horror have been a staple of fairy tales. But until a few decades ago, vampires weren't in many children's books (except for comic books).

Then, in 1979, the children's novel *Bunnicula*, by Deborah and James Howe, came along with a fresh take on vampires. The main character is a bunny. Instead of drinking blood, he sucks the juice from vegetables. His housemates, a dog and cat, become suspicious of his odd behavior. Convinced he is dangerous, Chester the cat tries to ward him off with garlic. He even tries killing the poor bunny by driving a stake through his heart. (Luckily, he mistakes "stake" for "steak" and uses a piece of meat.) Chester is so distracted by Bunnicula's eccentricities that he winds up having to go to a pet psychiatrist. Harold the dog, however, accepts the bunny for who he is: a vegetarian vampire. The book kicked off a series of Bunnicula books.

The following decade saw the release of more vampire books for kids. C. D. Bitesky, popular author of

POPULAR VAMPIRE SYMBOLS

Vampire lore contains many symbols. Did you ever wonder where these came from? Here are a few explanations:

- **Garlic.** Historically, people have used strong scents such as garlic to ward off the smell of death and disease, which were associated with evil spirits. In time, garlic was thought to ward off evil spirits in general, such as vampires.

- **Bats.** Real vampire bats suck the blood of animals, often biting their necks or shoulders. The Mayan camazotz was a mythic creature believed to kill dying men. In *Dracula*, the count is seen as a bat outside his victims' windows.

- **Stakes.** Folklore dictates that vampires be killed by driving a stake through the heart, severing the head, burning the body, or burning the heart.

- **Coffins.** In folklore, vampires are thought to rise from the dead. So it makes sense that they would sleep in coffins. Bram Stoker introduced the idea of vampires sleeping in coffins inside their own homes.

- **Fangs.** Some folklore depicts vampires tearing at their victim's flesh. But *Varney the Vampire* was one of the first novels to mention that vampires have fangs.

- **Tuxedos.** When *Dracula* was performed as a play in 1924, the title character dressed in a tuxedo and cape, which was later copied in movies about Dracula.

James Howe, signing books at BookExpo America 2006, and Deborah Howe wrote *Bunnicula: A Rabbit Tale of Mystery*. It is about a vegetarian vampire bunny.

the Fifth Grade Monsters series, wrote the vampire book *How to Be a Vampire in One Easy Lesson*. Vampires have since become a staple in children's Halloween picture books. Recently, *The Little Vampire*, a comic book–style picture book by Joann Sfar that was originally published in France, has become popular in the United States, too. In it, Little Vampire is the voice of reason among both his monster friends and his human sidekick, Michael.

In picture books, vampires haven't exactly taken the world by storm. However, in middle grade books, the undead have enjoyed much of the same popularity as they have among YA readers.

Middle grade novels are written for a slightly younger audience than YA books—third graders to eighth graders, rather than high school students. They're typically less edgy and have younger characters. There is some crossover in readership. *The Chronicles of Vladimir Tod*, for instance, begins with an eighth grade character, but follows him into high school. The Twilight series, though written about teenagers, is less edgy than many YA books. It has an audience as young as elementary school.

Popular middle grade vampire series don't usually focus on romance, as many—but not all—YA vampire books have. Instead, they tend toward mystery, suspense, and horror. In some, such as *Cirque du Freak* and *The*

John C. Reilly played the vampire Larten Crepsley in the 2009 movie *Cirque du Freak: The Vampire's Assistant*, based on the popular book series.

Vampire Plagues, the main characters are outsiders looking in on a vampire world—at least in the beginning. In others, such as *The Chronicles of Vladimir Tod*, *Vampire Island*, and *The Reformed Vampire Support Group*, the stories are told by the vampires themselves.

Beginning in 2003, the Cirque du Freak series has told the spooky tale of a boy who makes a deal with a vampire. The book begins with Darren Shan (both the main character and the pen name of the author) and his friend Steve attending a clandestine freak show. This isn't any ordinary freak show. It features a wolf-man who bites a woman's hand off, for instance. After seeing a special spider perform in the show, Darren steals it from its vampire trainer, Larten Crepsley. The poisonous spider bites Steve, but Darren doesn't tell the doctors what happened. Instead, with Steve on his deathbed, Darren makes a deal with the vampire to save Steve. The series, a mixture of horror and action, was made into a movie.

The Chronicles of Vladimir Tod follows Vlad, a half-vampire, through junior high and high school, as he lives on donated blood that his aunt smuggles home from the hospital. At the beginning of the series, his parents have died in a fire, his teacher has gone missing, and Vlad fears that his new substitute teacher is to blame for all this. As the series continues, he has a harder time resisting fresh human blood—putting his loved ones at risk. Through it all, Vlad is far from the smooth, cool vampire in other books. He is bullied, awkward around girls, and struggles to fit in. But in spite of his problems at school, he might grow up to rule Elesia—the vampire world.

On the lighter side, the My Sister the Vampire series is about long-lost sisters who discover that they are identical twins—only one of them is a vampire. *Vampire Island*, by Adele Griffin, follows the Livingston siblings—vampires from the Old World—as they try to fit in among the humans of New York.

Whether written for middle grade students, teenagers, children, or adults, today's vampires in literature tend to reflect—or exaggerate—our human emotions. For middle grade students, the vampires often struggle with fitting in. For teenagers, they represent uncertainty about who they are and a yearning for true love. For children, they represent the need to feel unique yet still loved for who they are.

Then, there are the bad guy vampires. They represent our fears. In *The Vampyre* and *Dracula*, manipulative aristocrats hurt those the protagonist loves. In *'Salem's Lot*, an evil visitor turns a seemingly peaceful

I Am Legend, starring Will Smith, was based on Richard Matheson's 1954 novel of the same title. The book is set in what was then the future, 1976.

town upside down. In *I Am Legend*, vampirism spreads like a plague. And in most books, vampires, like so many sinister creatures, only come out at night. The fear that we won't be able to protect our loved ones, the fear that we are not as safe as we think, the fear of disease, and the fear of the dark: these weigh on all of us. Historically, vampires have been used to explain these fears.

Nearly every culture has dangerous vampires in its folklore. But as time passed, authors weren't content to see vampires as monsters. They wanted them to be more like humans. With feelings. And a sense of good and evil. Why? Perhaps because people no longer needed vampires to explain disease and death, since they were now understood scientifically. But authors still wanted to express star-crossed love, loneliness, and the feeling of being different. So they wrote about vampires in a new way. They gave them a human heart. Well, some of them anyway. For those who like their vampires to have bite, there are still some of those around, too.

1732

A report is released about Arnold Paole, a suspected vampire in Serbia. Magazines pick up the story, spreading the lore to England.

1819

Englishman John Polidori's *The Vampyre* is published in the *New Monthly Magazine*.

1840s

Varney the Vampire, written by James Malcolm Rymer, comes out in chapter installments, known as penny dreadfuls.

1847

Bram Stoker is born.

1872

Carmilla, by Sheridan Le Fanu, is published, featuring a female vampire.

1897

Bram Stoker's *Dracula* is published.

1922

F. W. Murnau, a German filmmaker, makes *Nosferatu: A Symphony of Horror*, an unauthorized film adaptation of *Dracula*.

1930s

Bram's wife, Florence Stoker, sells the *Dracula* movie rights to Universal, which makes a film starring Bela Lugosi.

1933

Max Gaines creates the first comic book, *Funnies on Parade*.

1950

EC Comics publishes *The Crypt of Terror*, *The Vault of Horror*, and *The Haunt of Fear*, the first horror comic books. They feature gruesome vampires.

1954

Comic book publishers cut back on violent themes by establishing the Comics Code. It bans all horror, including vampires.

1975

Stephen King's *'Salem's Lot* brings a Dracula-type vampire to modern America.

1976

Anne Rice's *Interview with the Vampire* introduces a vampire with a human heart.

1979

Bunnicula, a children's novel by Deborah and James Howe, features a vegetarian bunny vampire.

1991

L. J. Smith's Vampire Diaries series introduces teenage readers to the romantic vampire.

1993

Linda Lael Miller writes one of the first vampire romance novels, beginning a trend that takes the publishing world by storm.

1997

The *Buffy the Vampire Slayer* television show, based on the 1992 movie, premieres, ushering in a wealth of Buffy books.

2003

The Cirque du Freak series begins telling the spooky tale of a boy who makes a deal with a vampire.

2005

Twilight is published.

2008

Charlaine Harris's Sookie Stackhouse novels become the HBO drama *True Blood*.

2009

The Vampire Diaries becomes a CW television series.

2010

The third Twilight movie, *Eclipse*, hits theaters.

aristocrat A member of the upper class who has certain refined manner-
isms, tastes, and moral values associated with that class.

camazotz A Latin American mythical creature with a male body, a bat
head, and a thirst for blood.

Carmilla The title character of an 1872 vampire novel by Sheridan Le Fanu.

comic book A magazine-type publication with stories written in comic-
strip style.

Comics Code Guidelines set by comic book publishers to decrease violence in their stories and illustrations.

dhampir A creature with one vampire parent and one human parent, making him or her a half-vampire.

Dracula The title character of Bram Stoker's 1897 horror novel. Also, a
fifteenth-century Walachian ruler known for his fierce battle skills
and for impaling his enemies.

EC Comics The first comic book publisher to produce all-horror
comic books.

gothic novel A style of fiction that features supernatural elements such as
ghosts and vampires, spooky settings such as castles, and dark themes.

graphic novel A book written and illustrated with words and captions—in
comic-book style.

horror novel A novel designed to terrify the reader by exploring the dark
side of the imagination.

manga Japanese comic books or graphic novels.

Nosferatu A 1922 German film that was an unauthorized adaptation
of *Dracula*.

plague A contagious disease that spreads to become an epidemic.

pulp fiction A type of book or magazine that offered readers entertaining stories for a cheap price.

romance novel A book in which a hero and heroine overcome obstacles to be together in the end.

tuberculosis A contagious bacterial disease that infects the lungs and other organs.

vampire A dead human who must drink blood for nutrition and may have superhuman abilities and a tendency to be evil.

vampyre An alternate spelling of "vampire" and the title of the first modern vampire story, by John Polidori.

Bram Stoker Memorial Association

Penthouse North, Suite 145

29 Washington Square West

New York, NY 10011-9180

Web site: http://www.benecke.com/stoker.html

This association celebrates *Dracula* and Bram Stoker.

Bram Stoker Society

Regent House

Trinity College

Dublin 2, Ireland

The Bram Stoker Society is dedicated to the study of the author and is based in his native Ireland.

Canadian Children's Book Centre

Suite 101, 40 Orchard View Boulevard

Toronto, ON M4R 1B9

Canada

(416) 975-0010

Web site: http://www.bookcentre.ca

This center focuses on Canadian books written for children.

Comic-Con International

P.O. Box 128458

San Diego, CA 92112-8458

(619) 491-2475

Web site: http://www.comic-con.org

This conference showcases comic books and comic-related material.

Horror Writers Association

244 Fifth Avenue, Suite 2767

New York, NY 10001

Web site: http://www.horror.org
This association is for both established and aspiring horror writers.

Transylvania Society of Dracula

Canadian Chapter, TSD

230–397 Front Street West

Toronto, ON M5V 3S1

Canada

Web site: http://www.blooferland.com/tsd.html
This society is dedicated to the study of all things Dracula.

WEB SITES

Due to the changing nature of Internet links, Rosen Publishing has developed an online list of Web sites related to the subject of this book. This site is updated regularly. Please use this link to access the list:

http://www.rosenlinks.com/vamp/vil

Brewer, Heather. *The Chronicles of Vladimir Tod: Eighth Grade Bites*. New York, NY: Dutton, 2008.

Goldberg, Enid, and Norman Itzkowitz. *Vlad the Impaler: The Real Count Dracula*. New York, NY: Franklin Watts, 2009.

Guiley, Rosemary. *The Encyclopedia of Vampires, Werewolves, and Other Monsters*. New York, NY: Checkmark Books, 2004.

McNally, Raymond, and Radu Florescu. *In Search of Dracula: The History of Dracula and Vampires Completely Revised*. New York, NY: Mariner Books, 1994.

Otfinoski, Steven. *Bram Stoker: The Man Who Wrote Dracula*. New York, NY: Scholastic, 2005.

Polidori, John. *The Vampyre*. Charleston, SC: Forgotten Books, 2008.

Schreiber, Ellen. *Vampire Kisses*. New York, NY: HarperCollins, 2003.

Spaite, Arjean, and Rick Southerland. *Everything Vampire Book*. Avon, MA: Adams Media, 2009.

Stoker, Bram. *Dracula*. New York, NY: Penguin, 2007.

BIBLIOGRAPHY

Benson, Elizabeth. "Bats in South American Folklore and Art." *Bats Magazine*, Vol. 9, No. 1, Spring 1991. Retrieved January 29, 2010 (http://www.batcon.org/index.php/media-and-info/bats-archives.html?task=viewArticle&magArticleID=477).

Beresford, Matthew. *From Demons to Dracula: The Creation of the Modern Vampire Myth*. London, England: Reaktion Books, 2008.

Bookstove. "The Mysteries of Young Adult Literature." November 10, 2009. Retrieved January 27, 2010 (http://bookstove.com/children/the-mysteries-of-young-adult-literature).

Brewer, Heather. *The Chronicles of Vladimir Tod: Eighth Grade Bites*. New York, NY: Dutton, 2007.

Caine, Rachel. *Glass Houses*. New York, NY: Penguin, 2006.

Crosby, Cindy. "Interview with a Penitent: How Anne Rice Moved from Fascination with Vampires to Renewed Faith in Christ." *Christianity Today*, December 1, 2005. Retrieved January 18, 2010 (http://www.christianitytoday.com/ct/2005/december/11.50.html).

Diehl, Digby. *Tales from the Crypt: The Official Archives*. New York, NY: St. Martin's Press, 1996.

Donnelly, Shannon. "Stephen King's First Comic Book." *The Daily Beast*, October 25, 2009. Retrieved January 26, 2010 (http://www.thedailybeast.com/blogs-and-stories/2009-10-25/stephen-kings-new-chapter).

Griffin, Adele. *Vampire Island*. New York, NY: G. P. Putnam's Sons, 2007.

Hajdu, David. *The Ten-Cent Plague: The Great Comic-Book Scare and How It Changed America*. New York, NY: Farrar, Straus and Giroux, 2008.

Harris, Charlaine. *Dead Until Dark*. New York, NY: Recorded Books, 2007.

Howe, Deborah, and James Howe. *Bunnicula: A Rabbit-Tale of Mystery*. New York, NY: Atheneum, 1979.

Ikeda, Akihisa. *Rosario + Vampire*. (Vol. 1). Trans. Kaori Inoue. San Francisco, CA: Viz Media, 2008.

King, Stephen. *'Salem's Lot*. New York, NY: Simon and Schuster, 2004.

Mead, Richelle. *Vampire Academy*. New York, NY: Razorbill, 2007.

Melton, J. Gordon. *The Vampire Book: The Encyclopedia of the Undead*. Detroit, MI: Visible Ink Press, 1999.

Memmott, Carol. "Romance Fans: Vampires Are Just Our Type." *USA Today*, June 28, 2006. Retrieved January 27, 2010 (http://www.usatoday.com/life/books/news/2006-06-28-vampire-romance_x.htm).

Meyer, Stephenie. *New Moon*. New York, NY: Little, Brown, 2006.

Meyer, Stephenie. "The Story Behind Twilight." Stephenie Meyer Web site. Retrieved January 27, 2010 (http://www.stepheniemeyer.com).

Meyer, Stephenie. *Twilight*. New York, NY: Little, Brown, 2005.

Miller, Linda Lael. *Out of the Shadows*. New York, NY: Berkley Books, 1993.

Murgatroyd, Paul. *Mythical Monsters in Classical Literature*. London, England: Duckworth, 2007.

Otfinoski, Steven. *Bram Stoker: The Man Who Wrote Dracula*. New York, NY: Scholastic, 2005.

Polidori, John. *The Vampyre*. Salt Lake City, UT: Project Gutenberg, 2009. Retrieved January 25, 2010 (http://www.gutenberg.org/files/6087/6087-h/6087-h.htm).

Rice, Anne. "The Angels Among Us." *Parade*, December 20, 2009.

Rice, Anne. *Blood and Gold*. New York, NY: Random House, 2001.

Rice, Anne. *Interview with the Vampire*. New York, NY: Random House, 1995.

Rice, Anne. "To My Readers: On the Nature of My Earlier Works." Anne Rice Web site, August 15, 2007. Retrieved January 27, 2010 (http://www.annerice.com/Bookshelf-EarlierWorks.html).

Rook, Sebastian. *Vampire Plagues: London, 1850*. New York, NY: Scholastic, 2005.

Schreiber, Ellen. "Biography." Ellen Schreiber Web site. Retrieved January 28, 2010 (http://www.ellenschreiber.com/bio.htm).

Schreiber, Ellen. *Vampire Kisses*. New York, NY: HarperCollins, 2003.

Schreiber, Ellen, and Rem (illustrator). *Vampire Kisses: Blood Relatives*. New York, NY: HarperCollins/Los Angeles, CA: TokyoPop, 2007.

Sfar, Joann. *Little Vampire*. Trans. Alexis Siegel and Edward Gauvin. New York, NY: First Second, 2008.

Shan, Darren. *Cirque du Freak: A Living Nightmare*. New York, NY: Little, Brown, 2001.

Sledzik, Paul, and Nicholas Bellantoni. "Bioarcheological and Biocultural Evidence for the New England Vampire Folk Belief." *American Journal of Physical Anthropology*, No. 94, 1994. Retrieved January 27, 2010 (http://www.ceev.net/biocultural.pdf).

Smith, L. J. *The Vampire Diaries: The Awakening and the Struggle*. New York, NY: HarperTeen, 2007.

Spaite, Arjean, and Rick Southerland. *Everything Vampire Book*. Avon, MA: Adams Media, 2009.

Spratford, Becky Siegel, and Tammy Hennigh Clausen. *The Horror Readers' Advisory: The Librarian's Guide to Vampires, Killer*

Tomatoes, and Haunted Houses. Chicago, IL: American Library Association, 2004.

Springen, Karen. "Children's Books: An Angelic Autumn." *Publishers Weekly*, September 14, 2009. Retrieved January 27, 2010 (http://www.publishersweekly.com/article/CA6696288.html).

Stoker, Bram. *Dracula*. New York, NY: Penguin, 2007.

Thorn, Matt. "A History of Manga." Matt Thorn Web site, 2005. Retrieved January 26, 2010 (http://www.matt-thorn.com/mangagaku/history.html).

Westerfeld, Scott. *Peeps*. New York, NY: Penguin, 2005.

Index

ABOUT THE AUTHOR

Bridget Heos is the author of several nonfiction titles for Rosen Publishing and several nonfiction picture books. In researching this book, she read lots of vampire books—from the creepy to the funny and from classics to manga.

PHOTO CREDITS

Cover (right) Bryce Lankard/Getty Images; cover (left), pp. 12, 15 Hulton Archive/Getty Images; pp. 5, 42 © AP Images; p. 8 SSPL via Getty Images; p. 9 the Granger Collection, New York; p. 17 Imagno/Hulton Archive/Getty Images; p. 18 Shutterstock.com; p. 20 Warner Bros./Getty Images; p. 23 Blank Archives/Hulton Archive/Getty Images; p. 24 FPG/Hulton Archive/Getty Images; p. 26 SHNS photo courtesy Marvel Comics/Newscom; p. 30 Susan Aimee Weinik/Time & Life Pictures/Getty Images; p. 32 Gene Shaw/Time & Life Pictures/Getty Images; p. 34 Prashant Gupta/© HBO/Courtesy Everett Collection; p. 37 Andrew Eccles/© CW/Courtesy Everett Collection; p. 40 Martin Bureau/AFP/Getty Images; p. 45 Courtesy of Char Gwizdala; p. 46 David Lee/© Universal/Courtesy Everett Collection; p. 48 Claire Greenway/Getty Images; interior graphics (bats) adapted from Shutterstock.com.

Designer: Les Kanturek; Editor: Bethany Bryan;
Photo Researcher: Peter Tomlinson

FLICKA, RICKA, DICKA
AND THE NEW DOTTED DRESSES

FLICKA, RICKA, DICKA
AND THE NEW DOTTED DRESSES

BY MAJ LINDMAN

ALBERT WHITMAN & COMPANY
CHICAGO, ILLINOIS

Flicka, Ricka, and Dicka are three little girls who live in Sweden. The three little girls look very much alike. They have blue eyes and yellow curls, and they always wear dresses that are just alike.

The three little girls look very much alike.

One summer morning their mother said, "I have made new dotted dresses for you. Would you like to wear them today?"

Flicka said, "Oh yes! I like to wear new dresses."

Ricka said, "I love red dresses with big white dots."

Dicka said, "These dresses have white collars too!"

When the three little girls put on their new dotted dresses they ran outdoors to play.

"Be sure to keep your new dresses clean," Mother called as they ran through the meadow toward the woods.

Flicka and Dicka picked daisies. Ricka tried to catch a butterfly, but it flew just ahead of her. On and on it flew, and Ricka ran after it.

"We must remember to keep our new dotted dresses clean," said Flicka.

"Perhaps we had better take our flowers back to Mother," said Dicka.

But Ricka was running after the butterfly. On and on she ran. The sun was shining, the birds were singing, the daisies were blooming everywhere, and the three little girls were very happy in their new dotted dresses.

Ricka tried to catch a butterfly.

Suddenly Ricka stopped. Just where the meadow met the woods was a path. A little old woman was walking slowly along the path. She carried a load of firewood on her back. On her head was an old-fashioned hood. When she saw the three little girls she smiled.

Flicka, Ricka, and Dicka greeted her. "Good morning," they said. "May we help you with your heavy load?"

The little old woman smiled again. She let the load of firewood slip to the ground.

"Thank you, little girls," she said. "I am taking this wood to my cottage. The wood is very heavy, and I am tired. You are most kind."

A little old woman was walking slowly along the path.

Through the woods they started, to the little old woman's cottage.

When each little girl took all the wood she could carry, there was none left for the little old woman to carry. Flicka walked beside her on her right, and Ricka walked beside her on her left. Dicka walked close behind the little old woman.

Through the woods they started, to the little old woman's cottage.

"I am Flicka. These are my two sisters, Ricka and Dicka. We have on new dotted dresses," said the one little girl.

"Oh!" replied the little old woman. "Do you think you should carry the wood? Perhaps you will get your new dotted dresses dirty."

"Oh, Mother has always taught us to help people," said Flicka.

So Flicka, Ricka, and Dicka and the little old woman walked on through the woods. When they came to the end of the path they saw a red cottage. It had green shutters, and flowers were growing everywhere.

"What a pretty little house!" cried Ricka, as she put her load of wood near the door.

"Can we help you any other way?" asked Flicka.

Dicka thought about Mother and their new dotted dresses. "Perhaps we had better go home now," said she. But as she spoke she heard a loud "Moo-moo-moo." The sound came from behind the cottage.

"That's Masie," said the little old woman.

They saw a red cottage.

"Masie is my cow," she explained.

"Masie is my cow," she explained as she seated herself on the doorstep. "You may call me Aunt Helma. I am very tired, and there is so much to do. I need fresh water from the spring. The chickens should be fed, and I need potatoes for supper. They are down in the cellar."

As she spoke, Flicka ran to the spring and soon returned with two big pails of water that splashed on her dotted dress with every step.

Ricka brought the potatoes from the cellar in a big basket. But it was Dicka who fed the chickens.

"They are all white but one, aren't they, Aunt Helma?" she asked.

"Yes, Dicka," was the answer, "but the brown one lays the most eggs."

"Here, Masie, is your supper," she said.

"Aunt Helma, may we milk Masie?" asked Flicka.

"You may try," she smiled. "Masie is in the barn just behind the cottage. Here is a pail."

Flicka, Ricka, and Dicka ran to the barn.

Ricka seated herself on a little stool, and began to milk. When she had filled the pail full she carried it to the cottage while Dicka swept the floor.

Flicka carried sweet-smelling hay to the cow. "Here, Masie, is your supper," she said. "I hope you enjoy it. Aunt Helma was much too tired to milk you. Now good night."

Then back to the cottage they ran.

"We must feed the pig," said Flicka. "Aunt Helma has his supper here in the pail."

She ran toward the pigpen, pushed open the gate, and was about to empty the bucket into the trough when she heard Ricka and Dicka cry, "The pig is out!"

Out of the pen, across the yard, and through the flowers ran the pig, with Flicka, Ricka, and Dicka close behind. Flicka still carried the pig's supper in the pail.

Dicka fell down, but Flicka and Ricka ran on.

Aunt Helma stood watching. How she laughed when Ricka finally caught the pig.

Across the yard ran the pig.

Soon the three little girls sat down.

When the pig was back in the pen and
Aunt Helma herself had fastened the gate, she
said, "Flicka, Ricka, and Dicka, you must be
hungry. Come now. You may each have a cup
of Masie's fresh milk. Perhaps I can find some
cookies, too."

She put a gay cloth on the table and soon
the three little girls sat down.

"My, how good the milk is," said Flicka as
she drank every drop.

"I like these cookies!" said Ricka.

Perhaps Dicka was looking at the cookies.
Perhaps she was only tired, but in a moment
her milk had spilled all over her dress, her
socks, and her shoes.

"Oh, my new dotted dress is covered with milk," said Dicka, sobbing.

"Mine is all dirty, too," said Flicka. "Now we really must go, Aunt Helma. It is almost dark. I'm afraid Mother would be anxious."

"Thank you for all you have done, my dears," said Aunt Helma. "Come again soon."

Then off through the woods ran the three little girls. It grew dark. "If we climb over this fence," said Flicka, "we'll get home much sooner."

Over the fence climbed Dicka, still crying. But Ricka's dress caught on the fence as she climbed over, and she tore a big hole in it.

Ricka's dress caught on the fence.

"Oh dear," sobbed Ricka. "Now I've torn my new dotted dress."

But on they ran, through the woods, across the meadow to the door where Mother stood—looking and waiting.

When she saw her three little girls, she caught them in her arms. "Oh! Your dirty hands and faces, and your new dotted dresses!" she said. "Where have you been?"

Then Flicka, Ricka, and Dicka told her all about Aunt Helma.

Mother said quietly, "I have taught you always to help others. I am glad you were kind to Aunt Helma. You must be tired, so run along to bed. We'll do something about the dresses tomorrow!"

She caught them in her arms.

The three little girls washed their socks and their new dotted dresses.

Early the very next morning the three little girls washed their socks and their new dotted dresses. Ricka mended her dress very carefully before she washed it.

"I'm sorry our red dotted dresses aren't new any longer," said Flicka.

"But Mother was glad we were kind and helpful," said Dicka.

"Our dresses will always be pretty," added Ricka. "I wonder how Aunt Helma will get along. She really needs our help."

Mother smiled as she overheard them. Then she said understandingly, "Always help others, every way you can. But when next you help Aunt Helma, why not wear your overalls?"

"Our dresses will always be pretty," added Ricka.

The FLICKA, RICKA, DICKA BOOKS
By MAJ LINDMAN

Library of Congress Cataloging-in-Publication Data

Lindman, Maj. Flicka, Ricka, Dicka and the new dotted dresses / by Maj Lindman.
p. cm.
Summary: Three little girls get their new red dresses all
dirty while helping an old woman with her chores.
[1. Helpfulness—Fiction. 2. Triplets—Fiction. 3. Sweden—Fiction.]
I. Title.
PZ7.L659Flgn 2012
[E]dc23
2011035237

Printed in China
10 9 8 7 6 5 4 3 NP 22 21 20 19 18

Design by Stephanie Bart-Horvath

For more information about Albert Whitman & Company,
visit our website at www.albertwhitman.com.